ALCOHOL
AFFECTING LIVES

BY AMY C. REA

MOMENTUM

Published by The Child's World®
1980 Lookout Drive • Mankato, MN 56003-1705
800-599-READ • www.childsworld.com

Photographs ©: Andrii Butko/Shutterstock Images,
cover, 1; Red Line Editorial, 5; Shutterstock
Images, 6, 16, 25; iStockphoto, 9; Dusan Petkovic/
iStockphoto, 10; Featureflash Photo Agency/
Shutterstock Images, 12; Marc Duf/iStockphoto,
14; LightField Studios/Shutterstock Images, 19;
DGL Images/iStockphoto, 20; Arek Malang/
Shutterstock Images, 22; PR Image Factory/
Shutterstock Images, 24; Syda Productions/
Shutterstock Images, 26

ISBN 9781503844865 (Reinforced Library Binding)
ISBN 9781503846388 (Portable Document Format)
ISBN 9781503847576 (Online Multi-user eBook)
LCCN 2019957919

Printed in the United States of America

Some names and details have been changed
throughout this book to protect privacy.

CONTENTS

MOMENTUM

FAST FACTS

What It Is

► Alcohol is a drug substance found in hard liquor, beer, and wine. This substance can lead to **intoxication**. People who are intoxicated may behave differently than they do when they're not drinking.

How It's Used

► People drink alcohol. It is one of the most-used drug substances in the world, and it is often used in social settings.

Physical Effects

► Alcohol can cause sleepiness, blurred vision, and decreased reaction times. It can also lead to clumsiness, an upset stomach, and difficulty with physical senses (hearing, tasting, feeling, and speaking).

► When people who have been drinking for years quit, they can go through **withdrawal**. That may make them shaky, nauseated, and sweaty. They might have trouble sleeping or have seizures. People can even die from withdrawal.

Who Drinks Alcohol?

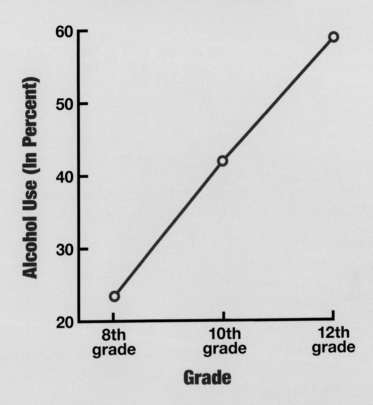

"Alcohol." *National Institute on Drug Abuse*, n.d., drugabuse.gov. Accessed 26 Nov. 2019.

Statistics from a 2018 national survey show that by the end of middle school, more than 20 percent of students have tried alcohol. By senior year of high school, that number jumps to nearly 60 percent of students who have used alcohol.

Mental Effects

► Alcohol can cause people to have a hard time paying attention, making good decisions, and thinking before they act.

CHAPTER ONE

DRINKING TOO MUCH

Alyssa stared out the window. She waited for her boyfriend, Eric, to pick her up. His car pulled into her parent's driveway, and the headlights lit up the night. Alyssa and Eric had been dating for three years, since they were both 14 years old.

Alyssa rushed outside and slid into the passenger seat. They headed for the movie theater. Their date started well. But after the movie, Eric wanted to go to a party at his friend's house. Alyssa felt her stomach clench with anxiety. Her hands began to sweat. She knew that if they went to the friend's house, Eric would start drinking alcohol. She suggested other things they could do, but Eric was determined. His friend's parents had left for the evening. He told Alyssa the party would be fun. She made him promise not to drink too much alcohol. When they first started dating, Eric only drank a little. Now he wanted to drink all of the time.

◄ **People can get very sick if they drink too much alcohol.**

At the party, Eric's friend poured alcohol into large glasses and mixed it with soda. Alyssa asked for two glasses with just soda. The friend made fun of her. She looked at Eric. He looked angry and told her not to be stupid.

It did not take long for Eric to finish his first drink. He asked his friend for another. Alyssa pulled his arm and reminded him that he had promised not to drink a lot. She had to shout so he could hear her over the loud music and laughter. Eric did not listen to her. Instead, he became angry. He yelled at her to stop bugging him about his drinking. If she did not stop picking at him, they would have to break up. Alyssa worried it would be her fault. Eric's friend laughed.

Alyssa did not want to break up. She loved Eric. But when he drank, he became a different person. Instead of being kind, he was mean. He yelled at her and called her names. He never did these things when he was **sober**.

Alyssa walked away from him and pulled out her phone to text her friend, Rachel. Rachel had just broken up with her boyfriend because of his drinking. Alyssa told Rachel what was happening at the party. Alyssa could see that Eric was getting a third drink. She heard that his words were slurring, or running together. It was hard to understand what he was saying.

▲ **When people drink too much alcohol, they may speak and act differently than they normally do.**

She worried about getting him home. It would not be safe for Eric to drive. Alyssa did not have a driver's license yet, so she could not drive them either.

Rachel agreed to drive Alyssa and Eric home. Rachel wanted to help her friend, since she knew what Alyssa was going through. Rachel asked if Alyssa would attend a meeting with her.

▲ **People who have loved ones with alcohol addictions can attend meetings to share stories and learn more about addiction.**

The meeting was for people with alcohol **addictions** and people who know people with alcohol addictions. Alyssa agreed. She wanted to help Eric. She hoped the meeting would give her ideas on how to do that.

The next morning, Rachel took Alyssa to a community center, where the meeting was held. They met in a small basement room with a circle of red plastic chairs. Alyssa listened as other people talked about their drinking. She learned that many of them had tried to stop drinking alcohol but could not. Several did not believe they had a problem, just like Eric.

When it was her time to talk, Alyssa was nervous. But the others listened. She was able to talk about how nice Eric was when he was sober. But when he drank, he either became very childish or very mean. People around her nodded. Many of them said they had seen that happen with people they knew. Hearing people talk about their experiences made her realize that it was harder to stop drinking alcohol than she thought. It was hard enough when someone really wanted to stop. Eric did not want to stop. She might not have any choice but to break up with him. Alyssa knew she couldn't force Eric to stop drinking. That was a decision he would have to make himself.

GETTING HELP

Trusted adults such as a parent, family member, doctor, teacher, school **counselor**, coach, or religious leader can help people find resources about addiction and give support. If a person is worried about someone else's drinking, they can reach out to organizations such as Al-Anon. This group is for family and friends of people who abuse alcohol. They get together to share stories and experiences. Doing this can help people feel less alone. Alateen is part of Al-Anon. Alateen has both online and in-person meetings for teens who have people with alcohol addictions in their lives.

CHAPTER TWO

LANA DEL REY'S JOURNEY

Lizzy Grant woke up one morning after graduating from high school. She wasn't at home. Her head ached. She felt like she might vomit. It was a terrible way to feel. But it wasn't the flu or some other illness. She had a **hangover** from drinking too much the night before. It was a feeling she knew well.

But this morning, she felt worse than usual. Lizzy wanted to go home, but she realized she didn't know where her car was. No matter where she looked, she couldn't find it. She felt like she had no control over her life.

Lizzy had started drinking alcohol at age 14. Her parents were so worried about her drinking that they sent her to a boarding school, where students live as well as go to school. Her parents thought a change in her environment would help her get sober. But it didn't work. She loved drinking and how it made her feel.

◄ **Lana Del Rey has struggled with alcohol addiction since she was 14.**

▲ **If someone drinks too much, he or she might wake up without any memories from the night before.**

When she was drinking alcohol, she felt happy and free. But when Lizzy woke up that morning and couldn't find her car, she saw that drinking was hurting her life.

As she looked for her car, Lizzy realized she wanted to find something else in life to be as passionate about as she was about drinking alcohol. She left the boarding school and went to **rehab**. While in rehab, she became interested in music.

As Lizzy worked on staying sober, she began writing music and made an album. That album did not do well. But when she changed her name to Lana Del Rey and recorded her first hit song, she became a popular musician.

In 2016, Lizzy was still sober, even though it was hard not to drink when she saw bad reviews of her work on the internet. At 18 years old, she began working at an **outreach** program for people suffering from drug and alcohol addictions in Brooklyn, New York. She helped people by working as an addiction outreach counselor. To her, that work was just as important—if not more important—than her music.

WHAT ALCOHOL DOES TO THE BODY

Lana Del Rey liked the way drinking alcohol made her feel. That can be the case for many people. But while alcohol can make people feel good for a short while, it can also lead to heart and liver damage, cancer, brain shrinkage, and hallucinations. Many of these are deadly. When people stop drinking alcohol, it's possible that their bodies can heal from the damage.

CHAPTER THREE

WHEN A PARENT DRINKS

Ella woke up in her dark room. It was late at night. She was warm and sleepy and not sure why she had woken up. There was a line of light under her closed door. Was her father still awake?

Ella got up quietly and eased her bedroom door open. Down the hall, the living room lights were still on. She could hear voices coming from the TV. She tiptoed to the living room and peered around the corner. Her father was on the couch. His head was tilted back and his eyes were closed. In his hand was a glass half-full of liquid. An empty alcohol bottle stood on the table next to the couch.

Ella knew what to do. This happened several times a week. She went over and carefully took the glass out of her father's hand and set it next to the bottle. She turned off the lamp and the TV.

◄ **Parents with alcohol addictions often have a hard time taking care of their kids.**

Ella wished her mother was not on the night shift at the hospital. Her mother could do all these things instead. Ella wondered if any of the other kids in her third-grade class had things like this happening at home.

The next morning, Ella woke to a quiet house. She got dressed and brushed her teeth. Her father's bedroom door was closed. That meant he had woken up at some point during the night and gone to bed.

Ella went to the kitchen and turned on the light. The dinner dishes from the night before were still on the table. She took them over to the sink, rinsed them off, and put them in the dishwasher. Then, she found a box of cereal in the cupboard and poured a bowl. But the milk container in the fridge was almost empty, so she had to eat the cereal mostly dry.

Ella also saw there was no lunch bag in the fridge. There was a loaf of bread on the counter. She would have to make another peanut butter sandwich and find an apple if there still was one. Ella was tired of peanut butter sandwiches. When she reached into the cupboard for the peanut butter, her hand felt a glass object. She pulled it out. Another empty wine bottle. When had her father drunk that?

Some parents can't function because of ▶ alcohol use. That may force their kids to step in and take care of the house.

Ella was sad. Mornings like this happened more and more often. Sometimes, she would come home from school to find her father already drinking. Ella had stopped asking to have friends over after school or on the weekends. She could never be sure if her father would be drinking or not. When he was drinking, he often slurred his words or said things that were embarrassing to Ella.

Her mother was gone often now. Ella felt not just sad, but scared. She knew what was happening with her father wasn't good. She had tried to talk to her mother, but she didn't listen. Her teacher had told the class at the beginning of the year that if anything was bothering them, they should tell her. Today, Ella decided she would tell her teacher about her father. She knew that talking about her home life would make her feel better. And her teacher might have some suggestions on how Ella's family could get help.

◄ **Kids with parents who misuse alcohol can get help from a trusted adult.**

CHAPTER FOUR

BECOMING SOBER

Andrew tried to watch television in his apartment, but he couldn't focus. He was covered in sweat, and his hand shook when he clicked the television remote. Andrew hadn't drunk alcohol for a while, and his body was going through withdrawal. He turned the television off, and the light from the screen went away. He sat in the dark. Andrew knew he should leave his apartment, but he didn't have a reason to. He had been kicked out of high school and he didn't have a job.

Andrew went to the kitchen and poured himself some soda. Then he mixed it with alcohol. He wanted to stop the pounding in his head. He thought he could fix how he was feeling by having a handful of drinks. But that only made him feel better for a short while.

◄ **After a night of drinking, someone may feel hungover. This can make it hard to focus on things.**

▲ **Someone who drinks often needs more alcohol to feel its effects.**

Andrew had been drinking alcohol since he was 12 years old. At first, it was something fun he did with his friends. But his friends didn't want to drink all the time. As they got older, they were focused on things like school and finding jobs. Andrew liked how drinking felt, so he continued doing it.

Drinking too much can result in alcohol poisoning. ▶ This is an emergency that requires doctors to get the alcohol out of someone's stomach.

▲ **Antabuse makes people feel sick when they drink alcohol, so they won't crave it as much.**

Now Andrew was 23, and he typically drank more than 50 drinks each weekend day. He needed more and more drinks to get the good feeling alcohol gave him. Andrew was building up a **tolerance**. Several of his friends told him he needed to get help, but he didn't believe them.

Andrew kept drinking alcohol, especially on the weekends. His best friends didn't like who Andrew became when he drank. They stopped hanging out with him. Andrew saw that alcohol was hurting his friendships.

Andrew finally realized he was drinking too much, so he went to the doctor. The doctor prescribed a drug called Antabuse. This meant the doctor gave Andrew permission to take the drug.

STAGES OF ADDICTION

There are stages that people may go through when becoming addicted to alcohol. Teens move through the stages more quickly than adults, so they are at a higher risk for addiction. If a teen's parent has an alcohol addiction, he would be more likely to develop one.

- Experimenting: Trying alcohol, often with friends, to see what it's like or to rebel against parents or other adults.
- Regular use: Drinking regularly and beginning to miss school or work, or avoiding friends and family.
- Problem: Drinking is the only important thing now. Nothing else is of interest.
- Addiction: Can't face daily life without alcohol.

Antabuse is made for people who have an addiction to alcohol. When people take Antabuse and then drink alcohol, they will vomit, feel chest and head pain, have blurred vision, and feel like they might faint. The drug takes effect right after people start drinking alcohol. It is meant to stop them from drinking. Even though the Antabuse made him sick when he drank alcohol, Andrew did it anyway.

Andrew didn't feel good when he drank, but it kept him from feeling bad about his life. He did not have close friends anymore. His father encouraged him to drink. His father was dependent on alcohol too, and he wanted Andrew to drink with him. Andrew nearly died twice. Once, he collapsed at a concert and woke up in the hospital. The second time, he was at a dance club and his heart stopped. Paramedics had to bring him back to life. Paramedics are people who respond to emergencies.

It was not until Andrew turned 31 years old that he found a reason to stop drinking. He enrolled at a school for sign writing, which taught him to paint words on signs in different styles. He loved the work. But when he drank too much, he could not keep his hands steady enough to do good work. He realized that he would have to stop drinking alcohol if he wanted to succeed.

Quitting drinking was hard. Andrew **relapsed** several times in the first year. But he was always determined to get back on track.

He worked with many support groups that helped him safely stop using alcohol. After a year, Andrew found he could resist the urge to drink. More importantly, he liked who he'd become when he was sober. He had made a close friend in sign-writing class. His friend also sobered up, and they helped each other. One year later, Andrew didn't miss the way he felt when he was drinking alcohol. Being sober and healthy felt so much better.

THINK ABOUT IT

► People over the age of 21 can legally drink alcohol. Why do you think alcohol is legal, even though it can lead to addiction?
► Many car accidents happen when people who have been drinking try to drive. Why would someone try to drive after drinking if it is dangerous?
► Addiction is a serious disease. How can a person avoid developing an addiction?

GLOSSARY

addiction (uh-DIK-shun): An addiction is a very strong need to do or have something regularly. People who feel they need to drink alcohol may have an addiction.

counselor (KOWN-suh-lur): A counselor is a person who offers advice. Many people visit a counselor for help handling their addiction.

hangover (HANG-oh-vur): A person has a hangover when he or she is sick from drinking too much alcohol the day before. After a night of drinking, someone may wake up with a hangover.

intoxication (in-tok-suh-KAY-shun): Intoxication occurs when people drink so much that they can't think or behave normally. Heavy drinking can cause someone to be in a state of intoxication.

outreach (OWT-reech): Outreach is the act of bringing information to people. The singer worked for an addiction outreach program.

rehab (REE-hab): Rehab is a type of treatment for drug abuse. Most rehab centers have strict rules for patients.

relapse (REE-laps): Relapse occurs when a person who has an addiction had stopped using the drug, but then starts using again. The student experienced a relapse when she drank at a party.

sober (SOH-bur): A person who is sober is no longer using drugs or alcohol. Staying sober after rehab can be very difficult.

tolerance (TOL-ur-uhnss): Someone who drinks a lot of alcohol builds up a tolerance and has to drink more to feel its effects. The teenager had a high alcohol tolerance.

withdrawal (with-DRAWL): Withdrawal happens when someone who drinks experiences negative effects after quitting. The father went through withdrawal.

TO LEARN MORE

BOOKS

Paris, Stephanie Herweck. *Drugs and Alcohol*.
Huntington Beach, CA: Teacher Created Materials, 2013.

Sheff, David. *High: Everything You Want to Know About Drugs,
Alcohol, and Addiction*. Boston, MA: Houghton Mifflin Harcourt, 2018.

Thiel, Kristin. *The Dangers of Alcohol*.
New York, NY: PowerKids Press, 2020.

WEBSITES

Visit our website for links about addiction
to alcohol: **childsworld.com/links**

*Note to Parents, Teachers, and Librarians: We routinely verify our Web links to make
sure they are safe and active sites. So encourage your readers to check them out!*

SELECTED BIBLIOGRAPHY

"Lana Del Rey: The Saddest, Baddest Diva in Rock." *Rolling
Stone*, 16 July 2014, rollingstone.com. Accessed 8 Oct. 2019.

Pietrangelo, Ann, and Kimberly Holland. "The Effects
of Alcohol on Your Body." *Healthline*, 9 June 2017,
healthline.com. Accessed 8 Oct. 2019.

"What Happens to Your Body When You Stop Drinking Alcohol."
WebMD, n.d., webmd.com. Accessed 20 Jan. 2020.

 INDEX

ABOUT THE AUTHOR

Amy C. Rea grew up in northern Minnesota and now lives in a Minneapolis suburb with her husband, two sons, and dog. She writes frequently about traveling around Minnesota.